"A rollicking read to sink your fangs into."
Young Telegraph

As a child, Alan Durant's favourite TV programme
was *The Munsters*. "I wanted to live in a family
like that," he says. "I liked my family and they
were interesting, but none of them had green skin
or fangs." Several years later, when he was a
grown-up author, he decided to write about his
childhood fantasy. Hence *Creepe Hall*. He has
since written two sequels, *Return to Creepe Hall*
and *Creepe Hall For Ever!* (1999). *Creepe Hall*
and *Return to Creepe Hall* are also available on
audio cassette. Among Alan's numerous other
books for young people are *Jake's Magic*; *Star
Quest: Voyage to the Greylon Galaxy*; *Spider
McDrew*; *Little Troll* and the Leggs United series,
as well as the picture books *Snake Supper*; *Mouse
Party*; *Big Fish Little Fish* and *Angus Rides the
Goods Train*. He has also written several books
for older children, including *Blood* and *Publish
or Die*, and compiled *The Kingfisher Book of
Vampire and Werewolf Stories*. He lives in a fairly
ordinary house just south of London with his
wife, three young children, cat and a garden shed
in which he does all his writing.

Books by the same author

ALAN DURANT

Illustrations by
HUNT EMERSON

WALKER BOOKS
AND SUBSIDIARIES
LONDON · BOSTON · SYDNEY

To my brother Richard
and his family:
Alex, Matthew, Emily,
James, William and Catherine

First published 1995 by Walker Books Ltd
87 Vauxhall Walk, London SE11 5HJ

This edition published 1999

2 4 6 8 10 9 7 5 3 1

Text © 1995 Alan Durant
Illustrations © 1995 Hunt Emerson

This book has been typeset in Plantin.

Printed in England by Clays Ltd, St Ives plc

British Library Cataloguing in Publication Data
A catalogue record for this book
is available from the British Library.

ISBN 0-7445-6307-0

Contents

Chapter 1

In which Oliver arrives and is shocked

··

Oliver was not impressed. He'd been sitting
on the station forecourt for ten minutes and
there was still no sign of anyone coming to
collect him. He didn't want to be there
anyway. He'd much rather have been at home
in front of the TV, watching *Star Quest*. But
his parents had gone off on some crazy trek to
the Himalayas and so they'd sent him out
here, to the middle of nowhere, to stay with
distant relatives that he'd never even met.
They're bound to be a right lot of bores, he
thought gloomily. *They probably won't even
have a video machine.* And then, to make his
gloom complete, it started to rain. Great
splodgy wet drops fell on his head and
trickled down his neck.

He'd just braced himself to get up and run
for cover when something banged down on

his shoulder, like a thunderbolt, and sent him sprawling.

"Master Oliver, I presume!" The voice, too, was like thunder. It boomed from somewhere far above Oliver's head. Glancing sideways, the boy found himself face to foot with an enormous boot. Slowly Oliver raised his eyes up and up and up ... until they were staring into the face of a giant. The man must have been seven feet tall at least – and with the weirdest face Oliver had ever seen! None of its features seemed to match. One eye was wide open and higher than the other, which was no more than a slit; one ear was massive, like an elephant's, and the other no bigger than his own; the nose was flat and snout-like and the mouth seemed to stretch from ear to ear. It was a shocking sight.

"You are Master Oliver, are you not?" asked the giant. Oliver stared at him, wide-eyed.

"Y-y-yes," he stammered.

"Wonderful," said the giant. "I am so absolutely thrilled to meet you, don't you know." He bent down and offered Oliver a hand the size of a baseball glove. Oliver could just about shake one of his fingers.

"Mister Vladimir sent me to collect you," said the giant, picking up Oliver's heavy trunk as though it were made of paper. "The automobile is parked over there."

Oliver looked across the forecourt ... and got his second shock in as many minutes.

"Surely," he murmured, nodding at the only vehicle in sight, "you don't mean that."

"Exquisite, is it not?" boomed the giant. "One does not see such craftsmanship these days. Of course, even this is nothing compared to the gilded chariots of my youth."

"But," said Oliver, with some indignation, "it's a hearse."

"Certainly it's a hearse. What else would you expect a mortician to drive?"

"Mortician!" said Oliver, frowning. "That means you're an undertaker, doesn't it?"

"Ah, bright boy," said the giant with a proud grin. "Of course," he added, "I am only an assistant mortician. It is your uncle Vladimir who is the master."

"My uncle Vladimir," Oliver repeated. "I didn't know I had an uncle Vladimir. My parents just said I was going to stay with distant relatives."

"Well, you certainly have come a distance, though strictly speaking I suppose 'uncle' is just a term of convenience," said the giant.

"And are you my 'uncle' too?" asked Oliver a little sharply, for he was becoming impatient with all this riddling sort of talk. The giant opened the back of the hearse and tossed the trunk inside.

"Goodness gracious no," he chortled. "I am just the faithful retainer, don't you know." Then he frowned, with the startling result that his wide eye clammed shut and his slit eye popped open. "I must apologize for not introducing myself," he said. "My name is Rameses Phaniacus Ozymandias Tutankhamen the Ninth." Oliver gaped at him, speechless.

"But you," added the giant with a smile, "may call me 'Mummy'."

Anything less like his own mummy Oliver could hardly imagine, but the fact that this giant was only a servant – even if he was seven feet tall – made him feel a lot more at ease. If the place had servants, he thought as they drove along, then maybe it wouldn't be so bad – and into his mind came a picture of a pleasure palace, filled with all kinds of magical delights.

At that moment, the hearse rattled round a bend and the giant let out a huge sigh.

"There she is," he said, warmly. "Creepe Hall." Looking at the building ahead, Oliver's spirits sank like a spoon into porridge. Creepe Hall was not a pleasure palace; it was a dump, a heap. It stood – just – between a tall tumbling-down tower and a thick, scruffy wood, and looked about a million years old. The roof sagged in the middle, the chimneys were broken or missing and there was no sign of a television aerial, never mind a satellite dish. All the windows had shutters over them, although it was still daylight, and the place seemed to be totally deserted.

Inside was no better. The floors and walls were all made of dark, cheerless wood, there were cobwebs and cracks everywhere and the lighting was awful – just a few flickering lamps. And there was not a sign of anyone. It was Oliver's worst nightmare: what on earth would he do here for two whole weeks, he wondered bitterly as he followed Mummy up a huge marble staircase and along a dingy corridor. They stopped outside a large wooden door at the end.

"Your room, Master Oliver," said Mummy. He pushed the door and it opened with a terrible creak, as if it hadn't been oiled for centuries. "You will find your dinner jacket laid out on the bed. Dinner will be served in half an hour precisely." Then, before Oliver could say a word, the giant servant turned and was gone.

Chapter 2

In which Oliver
gets himself in a twist over
a bow-tie

The room was big – at least he could say *that*
for it – but half of it was taken up by the
bed. It was an enormous four-poster with
curtains and, like everything else he'd seen
around the place so far, looked as though it
ought to have been in a museum. The
mattress was hard and lumpy and not at all of
the standard that Oliver was used to. There
was no bedside light, just an old lamp, no
clock radio, no wash-basin and, worst of all,
there was no TV. This was very alarming,
for Oliver loved TV. He watched it in the
morning before school and when he got home
after school; during the holidays and at
weekends he often watched it all day long.
He had to have a TV.

What concerned Oliver even more at the
present moment, however, were the clothes

that were laid out at the end of the bed. They were weird – worse than school uniform. There was a black suit, a white shirt and a black bow-tie, the sort of gear his dad wore when he went to posh parties – his "penguin suit", he called it. But this was just dinner. Surely he wouldn't have to dress up in this stuff every night, would he? He'd look ridiculous. Well, he'd wear it tonight, but that was it. He'd tell them at dinner – if anyone turned up, of course.

Slowly and without enthusiasm, he exchanged his sweatshirt and jeans for the shirt and suit. They were a bit big, but at least they went on easily enough. The bow-tie, though, was a problem. There were no clasps, no poppers, no Velcro tabs. How on earth was he to fix it on? Tie it like a shoelace, he supposed, but that was much easier said than done. You needed eyes in the back of your head. What he really needed was a mirror, but the only one he could see was on the wall, high above him. It was large, ornate and oval-shaped, like a picture frame with no picture in it.

Oliver had to stand on tiptoe on a chair to see his reflection – and a pretty sorry sight it was too. The tie drooped around his neck like a broken propeller and, worse still, now he couldn't get his own knot undone.

"Oh, blast this thing!" he said. But the more he wrestled with the knot, the tighter it became.

"Damn *and* blast this thing!" he said, starting to feel really cross.

"Temper, temper!" said a voice behind him.

"Language!" said another. Oliver froze. He stared ahead of him into the mirror, searching the room behind with his eyes – first one way, then the other, up and down. A chilly feeling ran down his spine. There was no one there.

"Mirror, mirror on the wall," said the first voice.

"Who can't tie a bow-tie at all?" said the second voice. And then both voices giggled.

This time, Oliver turned around. Lying on

the bed, looking up at him, were two identical-looking girls, dressed in white. They must have been too low down for him to see in the mirror. But how had they got there? He hadn't heard anyone come in.

"You shouldn't stare," said one of the girls.

"It's rude," said the second.

"You'll be turned to stone," said the first.

"Or into Mummy," said the second. And she pulled such a hideous face that Oliver, startled, lost his balance and fell off the chair. He hit the floor with a loud thump.

"Ow," he said, picking himself up slowly and rubbing his knee. But the two girls were too busy cackling to pay him any attention.

"Have you quite finished?" Oliver asked crossly, limping a few steps, as though in great pain. The two girls stopped laughing and looked at him. Oliver was taken aback by just how alike they were. It was uncanny. They had the same deep blue eyes, the same ski slope noses, the same pale, white, skin – and not only was their hair the same colour, but exactly the same length. Each wore identical white hair ribbons, white dresses and white shoes.

"I expect," said the first girl, "you'd like to know who we are."

"We live here," said the second.

"We're your cousins," said the first.

"The twins," said the second.

"I'm Constance," said the first.

"I'm Candida," said the second.

"Con and Can," said Con.

"Can and Con," said Can. Oliver looked from one to the other.

"I'm Oliver," he said.

"We know," said Con.

"And we're delighted you've come," said Can.

"We haven't laughed so much in *ages*," said Con.

"Centuries," said Can.

"Well, you shouldn't laugh at someone who's in pain," Oliver said primly. "It's not nice." In response, Candida pulled another, even more hideous face.

The dinner gong sounded and Oliver jumped, which set the two girls giggling once more. Huffily, Oliver turned to the door.

"I'm going to dinner," he said, expecting the girls to follow him. But neither of them moved.

"Don't you think you should fix your tie first?" said Con with a huge grin. Oliver looked down gloomily at his drooping bow-tie.

"I can't," he said. "The thing won't tie."

"I'll do it for you, if you like," Con offered.

"No," said Can, "let me."

"I said it first," said Con.

"Don't care," said Can and she made a grab for the bow-tie. Con did the same, and, a moment later, Oliver found himself in the middle of a tug-of-war. His face grew redder and redder as the tie was pulled ever tighter round his neck by the two girls, each trying to yank the bow-tie away from the other. All Oliver could see, as he rolled his eyes desperately from side to side, were two hands and two sets of long, painted nails – one red and one black.

Finally, the tie split in half, sending the two girls tumbling in opposite directions with Oliver collapsing on top of them.

"You nearly strangled me," he gasped. "And look what you've done." Frowning, he held up the split bow-tie, which looked a very sorry sight indeed. "I'll be late for dinner now too," he grumbled.

"Don't worry," said Can chirpily.

"You can blame us," said Con.

The two girls picked themselves up off the floor and Constance took out another bow-tie from the wardrobe and fixed it on Oliver. Her sharp red talons stabbed him in the neck several times as she did so, but at least the thing was on finally.

"Doesn't your mum mind you growing your nails that long and painting them like that?" said Oliver as they were walking down the marble staircase. "I'm sure my mum would have a fit."

Candida laughed. "Boys don't have painted nails," she said.

"But if I were a girl..." said Oliver. "What I mean is, you're too young, aren't you?" This time both girls laughed.

"Well," said Oliver irritably, "how old are you?" Then added proudly, "I'm ten."

"I'm one hundred and seventy," said Can.

"I'm one hundred and seventy – and two minutes more than her," said Con.

Oliver sighed and wished more than ever that his parents had let him stay at home while they'd gone away. Having half-wit twin girl cousins was just about the final straw. Couldn't they be sensible about anything? Damien and Darren, the twins in his class at school, were a bit like that – always being silly. They said they had this magical ability which meant that each of them knew exactly what the other one was thinking. Telepathetic or something, they said it was. It was pathetic all right. Perhaps being a twin made your brain go funny so that you couldn't help telling stupid stories.

They'd now come to the great wooden doors which led into the dining hall. Constance put her talon fingers on the brass handles and then turned to Oliver. "If Papa looks cross," she said slowly, "just mention bats. All right?" Then, closely followed by Candida, she walked straight through the closed doors.

Chapter 3

In which Oliver gets some weird surprises

This "trick" with the door was, as it turned out, just the first of several surprises to be sprung on Oliver that evening at dinner. For a start, there was the room itself, with its huge table, shaped like a bat in flight and lit by three smoking candelabra. Then there was Uncle Vladimir. Oliver had never seen anyone quite like his new uncle before. Like Oliver, he wore a dinner jacket and bow-tie, but unlike Oliver, he looked entirely at ease in his outfit. His hair was immaculate and his face, with its long, well-shaped nose, was very impressive. What was so extraordinary about him, though, were his eyes, which glowed red like hot coals in the shadowy gloom. They made Oliver feel very uncomfortable. So much so, that he became completely tongue-tied.

Uncle Vladimir was cross at the cousins'

lateness, so Oliver, as instructed by the twins, mentioned bats.

"So what do you know about bats?" Uncle Vladimir asked fiercely and Oliver's mind went suddenly blank, staring into those burning eyes.

"They're made of willow, sir," he said at last, spouting the first thing that came into his head.

"You mean they're willowy, surely," Uncle Vladimir replied suavely. "Well, I suppose you could say so. Delicate is the description I myself would apply. What else can you tell me?" Too late, Oliver realized that he and his uncle were talking about different sorts of bats. Now all he could do was add to the misunderstanding.

"They're used for cricket – and to keep them in good condition you rub them with linseed oil," he said.

Uncle Vladimir's eyebrows lifted high with amazement. Then he shook his head.

"For crickets?" he sighed. "You are very

muddled, boy. Bats do eat crickets, I suppose, if they cannot find anything better. But I've never heard of this linseed oil. Rub it in, you say. Sounds very strange. Mummy, you must purchase some tomorrow. Now, boy, drink your soup."

Oliver had taken only a few mouthfuls of the red liquid (which looked, but did not taste at all, like tomato), when he got another surprise – the biggest so far. Across the table from him, a place had been laid and a bowl of soup put down, even though there was no one there. This had seemed strange to Oliver, but not half as strange as what he now saw. For suddenly from the chair opposite, which he'd supposed to have been empty, a head popped up, took a noisy slurp of soup and then disappeared again beneath the table. And why had this been so shocking? Because, unless Oliver's eyes were playing tricks on him, what he had just seen had been the black and white stripes and strong jaws of a badger!

A few moments later, with Oliver still

staring open-mouthed, spoon in the air, the badger creature returned. This time two paws appeared as well and grasped the table as the animal stuck its long snout into the bowl and slurped up the remainder of the soup. Then it raised its stripy head, catching sight of Oliver for the first time. It would have been difficult to say which of the two looked the more amazed. The badger froze, his dark eyes wide open.

It was Candida who broke the silence.

"This is Cousin Oliver," she said. "He's come to stay with us for a while. You needn't worry, though, he's really not half as odd as he looks." This was just too much for Oliver.

"Me, odd!" he exclaimed. "That's a badger!"

"Of course," Con said.

"*Very* clever," Can added.

"Oliver," Con said, "meet Werebadger."

On hearing its name, the creature opposite drew back its mouth into a form of grin and made a curious snuffling noise.

"He's very pleased to meet you," Candida interpreted. Then the creature disappeared once more, only to return a few moments later with a mouthful of worms, which he offered to Oliver. Oliver declined.

"Is this your pet?" he asked, unable quite to believe what he was seeing and a little disgusted as well.

"Our pet?" Constance queried.

"Certainly not," Candida said. "Werebadger's our brother."

"Your brother!" Oliver cried. Then he shook his head. Another silly joke, he thought.

At this point, a new voice spoke. "Perhaps *I* had better explain," it said. The voice seemed to come from the other end of the long table from Oliver. But it was so dark there that Oliver couldn't make out the speaker. *Being in this dining hall is like going for a ride on a ghost train*, he thought, and he wondered just how many more creatures there might be lurking unseen in the shadows.

"You have, I take it, heard of such a thing as a werewolf?" the invisible speaker continued.

"Well, yes," Oliver said, remembering a film called *An American Werewolf in London* that he had watched on video with a friend a few months before, when his parents had been safely out of the way. "They're people who turn into wolves at night – especially when there's a full moon, I think."

"Precisely," the voice said. "Well, a werebadger is a person who turns into a *badger* at night."

Oliver glanced quickly at Candida, then Constance, looking for the smile that would catch them out and prove this was all a big hoax. But there was none. His cousins were good at keeping a straight face, he'd give them that. Oliver turned back towards the dark end of the table.

"There's no such thing as a werewolf," he said firmly, deciding that it was time to show them that he was no fool. "Except in films.

And I've never, ever heard of a werebadger. I think you just made that up."

For an instant there was total, deathly silence in the hall ... and then howling laughter broke out all around the table. It was Uncle Vladimir's voice that brought it to a stop at last.

"No such thing as a werewolf, boy," he said. "Why, you'll be saying there's no such thing as a vampire next." Oliver was just about to make this very claim when he stopped himself and thought again. *That's just what they want me to do*, he said to himself. *This is all a big joke and they want me to rise to their bait, so that they can laugh at me. But I won't. I'll play along with their game.*

"Oh, a vampire is quite a different matter," he said, in an offhand sort of manner. "Everyone knows there are vampires. We've got one living in our shed at home."

"Really," Uncle Vladimir said and his eyes flashed in the darkness. "And what sex is this vampire, boy?"

"Female," Oliver said quickly.

Uncle Vladimir's eyes glowed. "This is most interesting. I must come and meet her some time," he said, drawing back his lips in a large grin which revealed two particularly fang-like teeth. "There are, alas, very few ladies left amongst us."

Later, lying in bed, Oliver could not make up his mind whether his cousins were the world's biggest practical jokers or just seriously weird. Either way, he was not encouraged. Two weeks of this and he'd go bonkers. *I wonder where Mum and Dad are now,* he thought, once again bemoaning the wrong they'd done him in sending him to a dump like Creepe Hall, where he didn't even have a TV in his room.

The wind whistled in the boarded-up chimney place and the heavy curtains fluttered at the window. Oliver pulled the covers right up to his chin and left his bedside lamp burning. Tomorrow, he said to himself, he'd demand a proper electric light. All these

candles and things were ridiculous. His eye-
lids drooped. Just before they closed
completely, though, he had a vague
impression of a dark figure, like a bat,
appearing at the window, in the gap between
the curtains, silhouetted against the moon...

Chapter 4

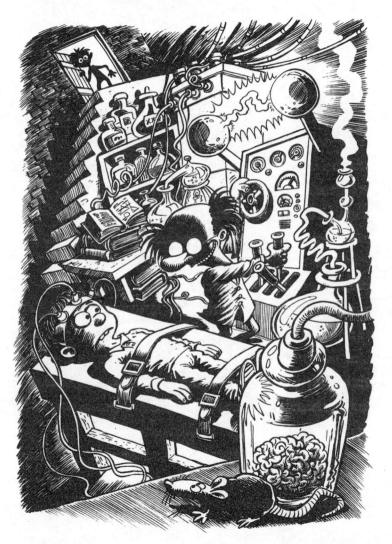

In which Oliver discovers Uncle Franklin at work

The next morning, when Oliver got up, the house was very quiet. The window shutters were still closed and there was no sign of anyone, upstairs or down. Surely it couldn't be *that* early, he thought. He couldn't be certain, though, because his watch appeared to have stopped. There was a big and noisy old grandfather clock in the hallway, but it wasn't much use, as the hands, curiously, went backwards. Anyway, his stomach told him it was time for breakfast, so he went in search of something to eat.

The kitchen at Creepe Hall was very different from the one at home. It was very old-fashioned, not high-tech at all. There was a solid old stove, a large sink and a wooden table, but there didn't seem to be any modern appliances: no split-level fan-assisted oven, no

microwave, no fridge-freezer, no dishwasher –
not even an electric kettle or toaster. Oliver
was wondering what on earth he would find
to eat in this ancient place when he became
aware of a strange rumbling and knocking. It
seemed to be coming from somewhere under
the floor. For a brief moment the floor
appeared to vibrate. Then it stopped. Then it
started again. Then it stopped. Oliver went
over to where the shaking had seemed
strongest, in one corner of the room. There
was a heavy door there and just as he put his
hand on the knob to pull it open, the
knocking started once more – louder this time
and getting louder still as the door creaked
open. Then the noise stopped again. And so
too did Oliver. For what he was now looking
down on was some kind of laboratory.

"Wow!" he exclaimed, amazed. He gazed
around the room, taking in the shelves of test-
tubes, flasks, jars and bottles full of different
coloured liquids, each with its own label. At
one end of the room was a massive glass panel

and a machine that looked a little like a huge car battery. Hundreds of wires joined this contraption to other pieces of machinery around the walls. There were things that pumped and things that whirred. One machine, covered in dials, lights and switches, appeared to be connected up to a boy, a bit older than Oliver, who was lying strapped to a couch in the centre of the room. In one corner of the room was a giant Mummy case and in another was a glass jar with something that looked like a human brain.

"Wow!" Oliver said again.

An elderly man turned round from what he was doing and looked up, rather vaguely, in Oliver's direction. He was bald and wearing very thick spectacles.

"Hello," he said. "Who's that?" He peered a little harder. "Ah, Oliver!" he exclaimed. "How nice to see you. You're just in time to assist me with this very important experiment. Come along." Then he turned away again. Oliver recognized the "invisible" voice that had spoken to him at dinner. Intrigued, he climbed down the spiral staircase into the laboratory.

The man seemed to have forgotten all about Oliver, though, for he carried on with his work and didn't look up. After a couple of minutes, Oliver coughed loudly.

"Excuse me," he said. The man turned, frowning.

"What? What? Who's that?" he said a little crossly. Then, it seemed, he remembered. "Oh, Oliver," he said warmly. Then his face went all blank and Oliver was afraid he was going to turn away and ignore him again.

"Are you my uncle too?" he asked quickly. The man stared at Oliver as though he were looking straight through him.

"Uncle," he said, running his hand over his smooth head as though searching for non-existent hair. "Yes, if you like. Why not? Uncle Franklin... You know Werebadger, of course."

So that's who the boy is, Oliver thought. "Hi,

Werebadger," he said chummily. "That was a great costume you had on last night. Brilliant. Really convincing."

The boy frowned at him. "C-costume?" he queried. "I d-don't know what you m-mean."

"The badger outfit," Oliver insisted. "You offered me some worms, remember?"

Werebadger blushed. "Oh," he said weakly.

"I thought I had explained to you already, Oliver," said Uncle Franklin tetchily. "Werebadger, here, was not dressed up as a badger, he *is* a badger. At night, that is. During the day, as you can see, he's a young chap like you – only rather shy, I might add, so please don't hurt his feelings with nonsense about badger costumes. Now, are you just going to stand there gawping or are you going to assist me with this experiment, umm?"

Oliver opened his mouth to protest, but Uncle Franklin had already returned to his work. *Oh well, I might as well go along with them*, Oliver thought. There was nothing else to do.

The experiment involved a lot of switch-pulling and dial-checking and note-taking. Uncle Franklin said he was measuring Werebadger's ever/never senses levels. Everyone had ever/never senses, he explained – you couldn't make a person without them. At one point, he threw a switch which made Werebadger's hair stand on end and his face go completely white. It was a bit alarming, but funny too, and Oliver laughed.

"Don't stand there giggling, boy," said Uncle Franklin testily. "There's serious work to be done." Then he reeled off a lot of figures, which Oliver quickly had to scribble down on a notepad.

The experiment lasted for nearly an hour and by the time it was over, Oliver's hand ached from all the writing he'd done – it was like being back at school, he thought. His stomach ached, too, from lack of breakfast. But he was curious as well.

"What exactly is the point of this experiment, Uncle Franklin?" he asked.

Uncle Franklin looked vague again. "Ah, well, Oliver, I suppose you could call it multiplication."

"Multiplication?" queried Oliver. The figures in the notebook didn't look anything like multiplication.

"Werebadger is a unique scientific phenomenon and I'm attempting to multiply him," said Uncle Franklin. "However, his ever/never senses are not like any I have come across before, so the experiment is proving rather long."

"How long has it been going on?" asked Oliver.

"Oh, about ten years, I should say, off and on, wouldn't you, Werebadger?"

"A-a-at l-l-least," stammered Werebadger. "L-longer, I should th-think."

"Longer than ten years!" Oliver exclaimed. "That means you started before I was born." He looked at Werebadger suspiciously. "How old are you, then?" he asked.

"One hundred and n-n-ninety-two,"

Werebadger replied.

"A mere youth," said Uncle Franklin.

Oliver looked from one to the other and sighed.

Chapter 5

In which Oliver learns some Creepe history and makes a decision

Oliver was disappointed. After a few days, the novelty of his new relatives wore off and he wished they'd just drop the games and act normally. They could keep proper hours, for a start; Oliver never saw the twins in daylight and Uncle Franklin and Werebadger spent all *their* time in the laboratory, getting, it seemed to Oliver, absolutely nowhere. There was lots of head-rubbing (which Oliver quickly discovered was Uncle Franklin's favourite thinking pose) and endless note-taking, but no action. Oliver very soon tired of the whole business. All he really wanted to do was watch TV (he'd already missed his favourite programme, *The Gloopers*, about an alien family living on Earth), but whenever he mentioned it he was met with blank stares or laughter, especially from the twins.

"Telly vision, telly vision," Can had taken to chanting at Oliver whenever she saw him. It was very irritating, he thought. Why she couldn't just tell him where it was, he did not know. (He refused to believe that the Creepes didn't have a TV. Everyone had a TV – Darren and Damien had one each and they only lived in a flat.) He'd have gone off looking for it himself, but most of the rooms, he soon discovered, were locked. Besides, he might run into Uncle Vladimir.

Uncle Vladimir made Oliver feel very uneasy. It was the burning red eyes that did it – and his alarming habit of popping up without any warning. On his second afternoon at Creepe Hall, Oliver had been walking along the corridor when, suddenly, as if out of thin air, Uncle Vladimir appeared, dressed all in black and looking every inch an undertaker.

"Ah, Oliver, my boy," he'd said in his low, lispy tone, opening his red eyes wide. Then he'd started talking of bats – which he now seemed to think Oliver had a particular interest in. Worst of all, Oliver was sure that Uncle Vladimir had misunderstood what he'd said about putting linseed oil on bats and had actually started putting it on himself! The smell when he'd walked by was quite appalling.

Although Mummy looked the most shocking of the inhabitants of Creepe Hall, he was actually, in Oliver's opinion, the least weird. He was the most friendly, too, and always had a kind word or a story to tell, no matter how busy he was. He said he was an Ancient Egyptian, risen from his tomb and patched up by Uncle Franklin. It was nonsense, of course, but the tales he told about the days of the Pharaohs were very entertaining. One afternoon, towards the middle of Oliver's first week, Mummy gave him a potted history of the Creepe family, while dusting the portraits in the dining hall.

"That is one of Mister Vladimir's oldest known ancestors, Ivan 'The Awful' Creepe," said Mummy, pointing at the first picture. It was of a man with the same burning eyes and sharp fangs as Uncle Vladimir, but who looked, if anything, even more sinister. "He had some very nasty habits, don't you know. He had a taste for peasants, used to roast them on a spit over the fire. Until they decided they'd finally had enough and did the same to him."

Quite a few of the Creepe family, apparently, had come to an untimely end. There was the tragic case of the first Werebadger, who had been shot and killed by poachers in the nearby wood. According to legend, Werebadger had turned back into a human as he died and scared the wits out of the poachers. Ever since, local people claimed, his ghost, in the form of a badger, walked the wood on full-moon nights looking for revenge. Then there was von Batty, whose portrait reminded Oliver of Uncle Franklin – only with hair. He was an absent-minded vampire who'd gone out for a bite one night and lost track of the time. Dawn had broken and caught the unfortunate Creepe out of his coffin. He'd been shrivelled up by the sun. Now the tower, in which he'd lived, was always in darkness.

The last picture Mummy came to was, in Oliver's opinion, by far the most striking. It was a portrait of Lady Eleanor, the twins' mother, who had died immediately after giving birth. She was beautiful. Dressed all in white, she had skin so pale and delicate you could almost see the bones underneath, and she had lovely dark eyes. Just looking at her picture brought tears to Mummy's eyes.

"She was such a sweet ghoul," he said, dabbing at his eyes with the duster. Then he drew from his pocket an enormous handkerchief, the size of a towel, and blew his nose with a trumpet that made the candelabra wobble. Oliver, who'd been brought up to believe that boys and men did not cry, coughed and made some remark about the weather.

That evening, after dinner, Oliver decided enough was enough. Instead of going to bed, as Uncle Vladimir instructed, he followed the twins to their room.

"Look," he said irritably. "I'm bored." The twins' response, as usual, was one of amusement.

"I'm your guest. You've got to entertain me," he continued.

"Entertain you?" queried Con.

"What *do* you mean?" said Can and she waggled her black-taloned fingers.

"Well, you know, show me where your TV is. Or at least play with me," said Oliver.

"Play with you?" said Con.

"Play what?" said Can.

"Well, you know, games," said Oliver and getting no response he continued, "well, like, like..." He hesitated for a few moments because he didn't actually play many games and the ones he did involve a computer or a video and TV screen, none of which he had so far located at Creepe Hall. "Like, er ...

cards," he said finally. "Or hide-and-seek or …
tennis or … riding bikes." It was hopeless.
The twins just stared at him as if he were a
total idiot.

"Well, what do you do all day?" he said with
more than a hint of frustration. "If you don't
play games or watch TV."

"Sleep, of course," said Con, which gave
Can the cue to yawn like a cat and waggle her
fingers some more.

"What do you do at night, then?" Oliver
persisted.

"We go out," said Con.

"If we can be bothered," Can added.
"Sometimes we just sleep and sleep." She
yawned again, which set the others yawning
too. But Oliver wasn't sleepy, he was very alert.

"Where do you go to when you go out?" he
asked.

"Here and there," said Con.

"There and here," said Can.

"Tonight," said Con, "we're going to the
woods."

"Yes," said Can, without enthusiasm. "It's Werebadger's choice. He always wants to go to the woods. He thinks that one night he'll meet the ghost of his old ancestor."

"Poor old Werebadger," said Con with a shake of the head.

"Ghosts," said Can dismissively.

"Can doesn't believe in ghosts," Con explained. "But I do – and so does Werebadger." Can made a sort of humphing sound. Oliver didn't have any time for ghosts either, except in books and films of course, but the idea of a night-time trip to the woods certainly did appeal to him, especially as there was no TV to watch.

"I'll come with you, then," he announced. Suddenly, the twins' eyes popped wide open.

"Oh no," said Con.

"Impossible," said Can.

"Why?" Oliver protested.

"Papa has forbidden it," said Con.

"He says you need your sleep," said Can. "But I think he's afraid you might scare the bats," she added, with a snigger.

"Linseed oil," said Con and the two girls collapsed into laughter.

"Look," said Oliver, "that was a misunderstanding. I was talking about cricket bats."

"Cricket bats!" Can exclaimed and laughed even more.

Oliver gave up. He turned on his heels and marched out of the room. He didn't care what Uncle Vladimir said (he didn't even know if the twins had spoken the truth about it) – he, Oliver Smythe-Rowland, had made up his mind: that night, when his cousins went to the woods, he was going with them.

T

Chapter 6

In which Oliver and his cousins have a weird encounter in the woods

It was a chilly night, but quite light. The moon was full and the stars were as bright as aeroplane lights against the black sky. It hadn't been easy staying awake so late – once or twice Oliver had thought longingly of his cosy bed – but he had been determined. He sat by the window, fully dressed and with his coat on, for what seemed like hours, watching for his cousins ... and at last he saw them. They were flitting their way across the grass, like white shadows, with Werebadger bounding along on all fours behind them. In a moment, Oliver was up and off down the stairs in pursuit... But even though he moved fast, by the time he got outside into the moonlight, the cousins were already disappearing into the wood. Oliver sprinted after them.

The wood was very dark; Oliver could hardly see a thing. He listened for any sound of his cousins, but he could hear none. There was no noise at all, not even a whisper of wind in the trees. Oliver shivered.

"Con! Can! Werebadger!" he called once, then again. But there was no reply. Looking down, he could just about make out a path, and he started to walk along it slowly. "It's all right for them, they're used to the darkness," he grumbled to himself. He felt sort of peeved that they hadn't waited for him – even though, of course, they hadn't actually known he was going to be here. Well, anyway, he'd find them. He stumbled on.

Suddenly, something fluttered, squeaking, close by his head, and made him jump. A bat. Just a bat. Immediately he thought of Uncle Vladimir. Mummy had said that Uncle Vladimir was a vampire. Oliver didn't believe it, of course, it was just another story, but...

He turned up the collar of his coat, covering up his neck, before moving on again into the darkness.

"Con! Can! Werebadger! I know you're in here," he called once more and with a lot more boldness than he actually felt. He was starting to wish he'd never come. With his cousins, it would have been an adventure, but on his own, it was just, well, lonely.

He'd only gone on a few more paces when another sound nearby brought him to a halt. The sound of voices: he'd found them! He was just about to call out when he stopped himself, thinking instead that he'd sneak up on his cousins and surprise them. Stealthily, he crept through the undergrowth... But it was he who got the surprise. For, peaking round the thick trunk of a tree, he saw that it wasn't his cousins at all. Crouching at the edge of a clearing, no more than a few yards away, were two men.

Oliver had a very good view of the men, because right overhead a gap in the wood's

roof let in a stream of white moonlight.
He didn't much like what he saw. The men
were very shabbily dressed with big beards
and mean faces. One of them was holding a
gun, while the other had a large hunting knife
in his belt and dangling from his hand were
two dead rabbits.

"Poachers!" Oliver said to himself.
"They're poachers." He didn't approve of
poachers. His disapproval quickly turned to
utter dismay, though, when, a moment later,
there was a rustle among the bushes and
something appeared in the moonlit clearing;
something black and white, standing on four
legs – a badger. Werebadger! He opened his
mouth to cry out a warning, but for a vital
instant, terror seemed to have taken away his
voice. By the time he got it back, it was too
late. His cry was drowned by the roar of the
poacher's gun. Oliver looked on in horror as
Werebadger went down...

The gunshot had barely faded, when out of
the bushes, like two white phantoms, came

Con and Can.

"What the...?" exclaimed the poacher with the knife, dropping his brace of rabbits. But the other poacher raised his gun menacingly. This time there was nothing wrong with Oliver's voice.

"Go back!" he shrieked. "Run!" The poacher with the gun spun round towards Oliver; his face wore an ugly snarl.

"What yer doin' there, yer loathsome pup," he hissed. "I'll have yer hide an' all." Oliver was scared, very scared. His knees were trembling. But he was very angry too.

"You're a murderer!" he cried. "That's what you are. You've murdered Werebadger."

At that very instant, as if on cue, there was more rustling among the bushes, and who should appear but Werebadger! At least it looked like Werebadger.

"Stone me," said the poacher with the knife. "There's another one of 'em."

"All the better," said the other poacher nastily, fingering his gun. "Two hides is better than one." He'd barely lifted the gun, though, when his – and all the others' – attention was taken by a sudden movement on the ground. To Oliver's amazement, the first Werebadger leapt to his feet – and a very terrifying sight he looked too, standing on his hind legs with his sharp claws raised and his powerful teeth bared... Without hesitation, the poacher with the gun aimed and fired. But unlike before, Werebadger didn't fall. He kept on moving slowly forward. *Bang!* went the poacher's gun again – but to no effect. On strode Werebadger, as though he were bullet-proof. And then, most astonishingly of all, he spoke.

"Wouldst thou dare spit fire at me, knave?" he growled fiercely.

This was too much for the poachers. The one with the knife looked already as if he were about to die of fright. His face was white as milk and his eyes were bulging like ping-pong balls. Now, he turned and fled. A split-second later, dropping his gun to the ground, the other poacher followed suit, closely chased by the snarling Werebadger.

"W-w-wait!" cried the second Werebadger. Then he, too, ran off.

Oliver stood still in shock for a minute or so, staring on at the place where the poachers and their pursuers had disappeared into the undergrowth. Then he looked round at the twins. Candida seemed particularly shaken.

"You look like you've seen a ghost," he said, without thinking.

"She has," Con said with a grin. And then Oliver realized... He recalled what Mummy had told him about the first Werebadger – the one who'd been killed by poachers, the one who was supposed to haunt the woods on nights of a full moon. Nights like tonight... He, Oliver Smythe-Rowland, no-nonsense champion of the real, who believed that vampires, werewolves, phantoms, ghouls, etc. existed only in books, films and on TV – he had seen a ghost! There could be no other explanation. And, if this were so, then what about all the rest? All those "stories" he'd been told and disbelieved, the stunts he'd dismissed as trickery...

Standing there with his cousins in the moonlight, just a bat's swoop from Creepe Hall, Oliver came to the certain conclusion that it was all true. And, what was more, he was glad.

Chapter 7

In which Oliver has a change of heart

··

There was no doubt about it, Oliver felt different. He wasn't exactly sure how or why, but somehow, after the experience in the woods, he felt changed, happier. On each of the next two nights, he went back to the woods with his cousins and had a great time. Just being with his cousins was a thrill; for it was a long time since he'd shared such active enjoyment. He watched TV with a friend occasionally, but that was hardly active – they just sat and stared. This was something else, and it was magic.

For Werebadger, on the other hand, these trips to the woods were a very serious matter. He hadn't managed to catch up with his ancestor that night they'd chased after the poachers, and he deeply regretted missing the opportunity to talk with him. He hoped, desperately, that the chance might come again. But, as yet, it hadn't, and coming home from their third excursion to the woods, the cousins ran into an angry Uncle Vladimir, returning from his own night-time wanderings. After that, Oliver didn't dare leave his room again at night.

To Oliver's delight, though, the twins decided that for the rest of their guest's stay, they'd change their habits and get up during the day. Oliver had grown very fond of his cousins and he didn't even mind when Con and Can teased him. It was just a shame that Werebadger wasn't free to play with them. But Uncle Franklin insisted on his presence in the laboratory all day every day, while he carried out his endless experiments. Whenever Oliver popped into the laboratory, Werebadger always said hello and smiled, but Oliver could tell that he wasn't very happy.

He, Oliver, was having lots of fun – and so were the twins. They really got into the games that Oliver taught them. The thing they liked best of all was playing cards. Oliver found an ancient pack in the dining hall, with very weird-looking kings, queens and jacks, and he showed the twins how to play Snap and Cheat (Con's favourite) and Beat Your Neighbour (or "Bite Your Neighbour", as Candida insisted on calling it). He was surprised, too, at how much he enjoyed the games. In return, the twins took Oliver around the house, exploring. Not only could they walk through walls, they also had a magical and very useful ability to open locked doors simply by staring at them. They tried to teach Oliver but, alas, without success – although once he swore he made a lock rattle.

The most exciting of these exploring expeditions was, without doubt, the afternoon that the twins took Oliver to von Batty's tower. Oliver had walked past the solid oak door a number of times and wondered what was behind it. Now, at last, he was to find out... The door had a huge old iron lock that was so rusty Con had to concentrate very,

very hard to get it open. At last, though, the lock clicked and Oliver pushed the heavy door open. It creaked noisily. Oliver held up the lamp he was carrying and led the way through to a gloomy spiral staircase, thick with cobwebs. They climbed and climbed (there must have been a hundred steps at least, Oliver thought) until finally they came to the top and the tower room.

The room was very dark and dusty and there were no windows. It had a funny, musty smell too, which reminded Oliver of his grandfather's wardrobe. But it was also, Oliver soon discovered, crammed full of fascinating objects – at least *he* thought they were fascinating; the twins didn't seem at all excited. They looked on with amusement as Oliver walked around the room, peering at things and exclaiming. He found a complete suit of armour, a stuffed bat in a glass case, a wind-up gramophone with a box of ancient records, an hour glass, a lift-up chest full of weird old clothes, a set of false fangs, a book

entitled *Eating Out in Transylvania*, a ...
coffin! He gasped and leapt back like a
startled frog straight into Candida. Then she
and Constance burst into laughter.

"Oh, Oliver," said Con. "Anyone would
think you'd never seen a coffin before."

"I haven't," said Oliver. "Not a real one."

"We've seen hundreds," boasted Can.

"Thousands," said Con.

"Yes, well," said Oliver, recovering from his
shock, "your dad's an undertaker, isn't he?"
Con glided over to the coffin.

"Do you want to see inside?" she asked.
Oliver wasn't sure that he did – an unpleasant
picture coming into his mind of a centuries-
old, decomposed Creepe. But Con's hand
was already on the lid of the coffin and lifting.
Oliver stared, cowering a little, as the lid
opened to reveal ... nothing. He sighed with
relief. The coffin was empty – well, almost. At
the bottom was a small sign, with scratchy old
writing, that read: *Out to luncheon. Back before
the sunrise.*

"Von Batty wrote that," said Con.

"But he never came back," said Can with unusual seriousness. Then, almost at once, she nodded at the coffin and added casually, "Have a go in it if you like."

Oliver shuddered. "No fear," he said. He looked around the room again and a thought came to him. "You know," he said enthusiastically, "this would make a really great den."

The twins looked at him as if he were completely mad.

"Why would a fox want to live up here?" said Con at last.

"No, not a fox's den," Oliver explained. "I mean this could be *our* den – you know, our special place." This idea appealed to the twins immensely and they quickly agreed.

"Let's tell Werebadger," Can said eagerly.

After that, the three of them visited the tower every day and often in the evenings too, when Werebadger, free at last from his labours, would join them. He looked sadder than ever now, though, Oliver noticed. He was very quiet too, and hardly even so much as snuffled. Oliver really wished that he could do something to make his cousin happier.

He was also becoming aware that there was someone else at Creepe Hall in need of help – and that was Mummy. For the first week or so of his stay, Oliver had looked upon the giant simply as a servant, albeit one who told good stories – and servants were there to serve, that was their job. As the days passed, however, Oliver came to see Mummy more as a friend and he could not help noticing how tired and pale he looked. He had so much to do, trying to keep Creepe Hall in order, and then he had to assist Uncle Vladimir with the undertaking – and Uncle Vladimir, Oliver was certain, was no easy master. Mummy's plight was brought dramatically to everyone's attention one night at supper, when he dropped the entire main course with a crash and a splash on the dining-hall floor. Uncle Vladimir's eyes flashed angrily in the candlelight, but Oliver quickly got up to help.

For the first time in his life, Oliver felt sorry for a grown-up – and the next day he made a momentous decision. He decided to give Mummy a hand with the household chores and he even managed to persuade the twins to help as well. The reason it was such a momentous decision was that Oliver had never so much as made his bed before; at home, everything was done for him. Now he and the twins were busy dusting, cleaning, washing and sweeping – and actually having quite a lot of fun doing it. For a while, anyway. Con and Can managed to turn doing the washing into a massive wet-clothes water battle and they had some great feather-duster "sword" fights. But it was very hard work too, and by the end of the day they were all exhausted.

"That's it," Can grumbled when they'd retired to the tower room. "I'm not doing any more. Just look at my nails." She held out one grimy hand to reveal a line of cracked or broken black nails.

"Mine too," said Con, inspecting her grubby red-nailed fingers.

"The real problem," a very tired Oliver told Mummy that evening, "is that this place just isn't equipped. You haven't even got electricity." Then he showed Mummy a list he'd made of essential domestic appliances: washing machine, tumble-drier, cooker, dishwasher, fridge-freezer, vacuum cleaner – and explained what all these things did.

"Alas, Mister Vladimir would never have anything like that in the house," said Mummy gloomily. "He detests newfangled things, don't you know. He would never agree to the purchase of such appliances, I fear."

It was then that Oliver had his brainwave – a killing-two-birds-with-one-stone sort of idea that would help both Mummy *and* Werebadger.

"I'll get Uncle Franklin to help us," he said.

Chapter 8

In which Uncle Franklin makes a useful contribution

....

Uncle Franklin was just completing stage 77a of experiment 198V/xf[i] in his Werebadger multiplication study. To Oliver it seemed just like all the other stages. Lying on the couch, Werebadger looked thoroughly miserable.

"A washing machine?" queried Uncle Franklin, when Oliver showed him his list. "What is wrong with a bath?"

"A w-washing machine is for w-washing c-clothes," said Werebadger timidly. "Isn't that s-so, Oliver?" Oliver nodded.

"And what's this vacuum cleaner?" Uncle Franklin asked, puzzled. "Why on earth would anyone want to clean a vacuum?"

Oliver spent the next hour explaining to an increasingly fascinated Uncle Franklin each of the machines on his list.

"What I was thinking," Oliver said, "was that perhaps we could make them, here in your laboratory. Werebadger wouldn't mind postponing the experiments on him for a bit, would you, Werebadger?"

"N-n-no, not at all," said Werebadger happily.

"And machines are sort of like human beings anyway, aren't they, in a way? So it would be like doing research, wouldn't it, Uncle Franklin, for your multiplication experiments?" Oliver looked at his uncle hopefully. Uncle Franklin ran his hand over his bald head and frowned.

"Hmmm," he murmured vaguely. "Hmmmmmm. Very interesting." For a moment, Oliver was afraid that his uncle's mind had wandered onto something else entirely. But then he looked down at Oliver and smiled.

"Right, my boy," he said. "Let's get to work!"
Uncle Franklin worked surprisingly fast.

The new project absorbed him totally, as the Werebadger experiments had before. For one whole night and day, he worked, without sleeping. Oliver didn't know how he did it. Werebadger didn't appear to sleep either – and seemed much happier already in his new role as assistant. In fact, he showed a real gift for seeing practical solutions that often didn't occur to Uncle Franklin's complicated mind. The vacuum cleaner – the first machine to be completed – was really as much Werebadger's as Uncle Franklin's creation.

The vacuum cleaner was very different from the hi-tech Hoover Oliver had at home, looking more like an electric brush with a large football attached. According to Uncle Franklin, however, the invention worked on exactly the same principles as any ordinary vacuum cleaner and he quoted a great many figures to prove it. Oliver, they all agreed, should have the privilege of trying out this new machine, as it had been his idea.

They all gathered in the long, carpeted

hallway – all, that is, except Uncle Vladimir, who was busy "embalming a customer" in his funeral parlour. In the absence of any electricity, Uncle Franklin had plugged the cleaner into the massive solar-powered generator that he had built in order to conduct his experiments.

"Are we ready?" Oliver asked.

"We're ready," said Uncle Franklin. Oliver flicked the switch and the vacuum cleaner roared into action. In fact, it raced away so fast that Oliver could hardly keep up with it. Down the hallway it zoomed, dragging Oliver along behind until ... WHAM! SMASH! CRASH! CRUNCH! The cleaner ran straight into the end wall – and, with a thud, Oliver followed it. Suddenly, everything went dark.

"Are you all right, Oliver?" said a voice that sounded like Constance's.

"Yes, I think so," said Oliver, vaguely. "But where am I?" He seemed to be inside a very black and dusty hole. Every time he opened his mouth, a piece of fluff popped in. And

then it dawned on him. He wasn't inside a
black hole at all. His head was inside a burst
football. A moment later, he could feel his
head being pulled upwards and then, all of a
sudden, the football was in the hands of the
twins and he was back in daylight once more.
It was still very dusty, though. He'd just
opened his mouth to say as much when a very
large bit of fluff slipped in and sent him into a
fit of choking.

Several slaps on the back and gulps of water
later, Oliver finally stopped spluttering. He
looked up to see Can and Con peering down
at him – each wearing a broad grin.

"Oh, Oliver," said Candida. "You are funny."

"Hilarious," agreed Constance and she bent
down and gave Oliver a kiss on the cheek.
"You must learn to go *through* the wall, you
know, it's much less painful."

The only one who wasn't amused was
Werebadger. He looked down mournfully at
the broken machine. "Wh-what a t-terrible
f-failure," he stuttered miserably. But Oliver

shook his head.

"Not at all, cousin," he said. "Look!" And he shook his head again, only much more vigorously this time, so that a cloud of dust and fluff flew off his hair. "See! If the cleaner had been a total failure, then the bag would have been empty and I wouldn't be all covered in rubbish. See how clean the carpet looks." They all looked back up the hallway in the direction that Oliver was pointing. It was true, a strip of spotless carpet showed the vacuum cleaner's path.

"Th-then it did work!" said Werebadger happily.

"Yes, indeed," said Uncle Franklin. "It just needs slowing down a bit, I should say."

"Oh, simply splendid, don't you know!" Mummy enthused.

"Three cheers for Uncle Franklin and Werebadger!" cried Con and Can, and they took Oliver's hands and did a little jig of delight.

Now new machines came thick and fast. In

no time at all, Uncle Franklin had supplied and installed a washing machine and tumble-drier, a split-level cooker and the biggest fridge-freezer Oliver had ever seen.

In fact, none of Uncle Franklin's inventions looked quite like anything Oliver had seen before, but then he had to admit that his drawings hadn't exactly been perfect. So it wasn't really surprising that they had the odd near disaster – like the flame from one of the cooker rings scorching the kitchen ceiling, or the flood that poured out of the washing machine until they plumbed in a waste pipe. The stuff worked in the end, though; that was the important thing. But even more important was that Werebadger was happy. He seemed, at last, to have pushed aside his disappointment at not talking to his ancestor in the woods. He talked lots now and hardly stammered at all.

Mummy was very happy too. "Absolutely top hole, don't you know," was his enthusiastic verdict on the new equipment. Uncle

Vladimir, however, was still to be convinced.

"In the name of Beezlebub, what is that!" he cried one evening when Oliver was vacuuming the hall. Oliver switched off the machine and looked up to the alarming sight of Uncle Vladimir hanging upside down from the chandelier, eyes blazing like lasers. He recovered quickly, though, and tried to persuade his uncle that the vacuum cleaner was in fact a sort of mechanical vampire bat, which sucked up dust rather than blood.

"I should say it looked more like an ostrich, boy," Uncle Vladimir retorted. But when, in another moment of inspiration, Oliver suggested giving his uncle's name to the new "species", a rare smile appeared on Uncle Vladimir's face.

"*Chiroptera vladimira,*" he lisped, grinning toothily. "Ummm, that does have a certain ring to it, I must confess." Oliver smiled too. At last, he'd done something that met with his uncle's approval. His happiness at Creepe Hall was just about complete.

Chapter 9

In which TV gets the thumbs down and Oliver says farewell

The days passed. Uncle Franklin, flushed with the success of his practical creations and wishing also to do something for Oliver, decided to try his hand at some leisure machines. He was particularly taken with the idea of television, which he had heard Oliver talk about so much. The strange thing was, though, that Oliver no longer had any desire to watch TV – not even *The Gloopers*. His new relatives were so interesting and so much fun it was sort of like being in a TV programme anyway – only better, much better. In any case, Uncle Franklin's attempts to create a television were not successful. The set he produced was plagued with a sort of hissing interference and all the programmes seemed to be in some strange foreign language.

"Um," said Uncle Franklin, rubbing his

bald head and looking more absent-minded than ever. "We appear to be tuned in to Transylvania. That's the problem of having a vampire in the family, I'm afraid. They tend to play havoc with the broadcasting signals." The twins sat watching the fuzzy screen for a while, looking very puzzled.

"Well, Oliver," said Can, at last, "if this is what you spend all your time doing at home, you must have a really dull life."

"It's not like this at home," said Oliver. "You can see the pictures clearly." But it was just a token defence and he quickly changed the subject to photography, having just remembered that he'd brought his camera with him to Creepe Hall and that it was about time he used it.

Getting his relatives to pose for him was no easy matter. It took a great deal of pleading to persuade them and even then Uncle Vladimir insisted on wearing dark glasses, although the sun wasn't at all bright, and the twins kept fidgeting. Oliver had taken only a couple of snaps before Werebadger whisked the camera out of his hand and suggested that he become the photographer – and Oliver was too amazed at his cousin's new boldness to argue. He got Mummy to drop the film into the chemist later that afternoon when he went shopping.

"Why do you want the chemist to see your pictures?" said Con.

"He doesn't even know you," said Can.

"The photographic process is very complex, my dears," Uncle Franklin interjected and then delivered a ten minute lecture on film development that left no one any the wiser – not even Oliver, who thought he knew a little about photography.

One thing Oliver certainly did know, although increasingly he tried not to think about it, was that the summer holidays were drawing to a close – and that meant so was his stay at Creepe Hall. On the afternoon after the photography session, the summons he'd once longed for, and now dreaded, arrived.

It came in the form of a postcard from his parents, requesting his return home the following day. Even though he was expecting it, the news was a shattering blow.

The twins were in the tower room when he told them. Con was playing a game of Patience (and cheating, as usual), while Can was walking round the room, balancing the false fangs on her head. At Oliver's words they stopped dead and went paler than ever.

"Oh," they said as one. There was an awkward, rather miserable silence and then Con said, softly, "We *will* miss you, Oliver."

"It just won't be the same without you," said Can, looking at the fangs in her hand as though they were the saddest thing she had ever set eyes on. Oliver himself had to bite his lip to stop the tears from coming.

"You will come back, won't you?" Con pleaded.

"Of course I will," said Oliver, trying to sound cheery. But cheery was the last thing he felt, and for the rest of the day he could hardly raise a smile. That night, in bed, he felt so sad that he cried.

His last day, though, wasn't as gloomy as he'd thought it would be. He spent the morning playing several games of cards with the twins, who made a big effort to be jolly. In the afternoon, Mummy made him a special farewell tea, the highlight of which was an enormous chocolate cake, shaped like Creepe Hall and with the words GOOD LUCK, OLIVER iced on it. It was the most wonderful cake Oliver had ever seen.

"It's great, Mummy," he enthused. Mummy smiled so broadly that his whole face became one enormous mouth.

"Oh, it's amazin' what one can do when one has a decent cookin' machine, don't you know," he said modestly.

"Ummm," agreed Uncle Vladimir, taking a large bite. "I could get my teeth into this sort of thing every day." He gave Oliver a big, toothy smile. "I must say, boy, that you have been a great asset to this house. Any time you wish to return, you can be sure you will be made most welcome." And at that, Oliver, too, had to grin.

His only disappointment was that Uncle Franklin and Werebadger didn't show up for the tea. They had been locked in the laboratory all day, leaving strict instructions that on no account were they to be disturbed. Oliver presumed that Uncle Franklin was involved in some new experiment and so he didn't really expect to see him or Werebadger again. But just as he'd climbed into the back of the hearse next to the twins and was raising his hand in farewell to Uncle Vladimir, a red-faced Werebadger appeared in the doorway.

"H-hold on!" he cried with only the very slightest of stammers. "Wait for me!"

"So here you are at last," lisped Uncle Vladimir. "What on earth have you been doing?"

"We have been creating something very special," panted Uncle Franklin, who had followed Werebadger out into the drive. His bald head was glowing and he looked unusually excited. "Show Oliver, Werebadger."

Werebadger stepped forward and handed Oliver something wrapped in a cloth. "This is for y-you, Oliver," he said happily.

Oliver removed the cloth and gasped.

"Wow," he said. In his hands was a magnificent bedside lamp, shaped like a full moon and with a host of glittering stars. At the bottom stood a smiling badger.

"It's so that when you go to b-bed at night you can think of us," said Werebadger.

"I will," said Oliver, "I will. Thank you, Werebadger. Thank you, Uncle Franklin. It's brilliant."

"It's but a small thing in comparison to what you have done for us," said Uncle Franklin. "We've yet to master the electrics, I'm afraid, but who knows, perhaps by the time you return..." Uncle Franklin's face suddenly took on the vague expression that Oliver had come to know so well. "You are going to come again, aren't you?"

"Of course, Uncle Franklin," said Oliver confidently. Then it was time to go.

The cousins spent the first part of the journey chatting excitedly about Oliver's gift. Then the talk turned to his stay and some of the things that had happened. They laughed about the bow-tie and the vacuum cleaner and relived again the thrilling encounter in the woods with Werebadger's ancestor and the poachers... But all of a sudden, Oliver felt very flat. It was a strange sort of bottomless-stomach feeling, a kind of homesickness, like he'd had when he'd first arrived at Creepe Hall – only now he was homesick *for* Creepe Hall. He felt so different now, not at all like the Oliver who'd arrived a couple of weeks before. He felt like he belonged at Creepe Hall. He just didn't want to go.

At last, having gone on a slight detour so that Oliver could collect his photographs from the chemist, the car arrived at the station. Mummy went round the back of the hearse to unload Oliver's trunk. Oliver recalled the afternoon of his arrival and the shock he'd got on first seeing his giant chauffeur. Now, as then, Mummy lifted the heavy trunk as though it were made of balsa wood and filled with feathers. He carried it onto the platform and saw that it was packed safely into the guard's van of the waiting train.

"Well, Master Oliver," he said, opening the carriage door, "I have to say, don't you know, that you've been a simply spiffin' guest." And he reached down a huge hand and squeezed Oliver's shoulder.

"It's been great," said Con.

"Brill," said Can, grinning. And they each kissed Oliver on the cheek.

"It's been m-most educational too," said Werebadger, who, Oliver noticed, was starting to sound very like Uncle Franklin.

"Do you *promise* you'll come back soon?" asked Con.

"I promise," said Oliver and, feeling his bottom lip start to quiver, quickly added, "I'll ask my parents if I can come and stay during the Christmas holidays."

"Is that soon?" asked Can.

"Very," said Oliver, though in truth it seemed at that moment to be years away.

A few moments later, Oliver was at the carriage window, waving as the train started to draw out of the station.

"Don't forget to write!" called Con.

"See you at Christmas!" cried Can.

"Yes, at Christmas!" Oliver echoed. "Bye!" And he waved frantically, until the train turned a corner and the platform was no longer in sight.

For a while he just sat rather sadly, thinking about how much he was going to miss his distant relatives. Then he suddenly remembered about the photographs. Eagerly, he took the bulky packet out of his coat pocket and opened it.

He could not believe his eyes! Hardly any of the photographs had come out properly. There were one or two of the house and gardens and a few of him – but in not a single one was there a Creepe to be seen. It was as though they had never been there at all. He turned again to the shots that Werebadger had taken. Oliver himself was there, clear enough, but there was no sign of the twins, who'd been standing on either side of him.

"It's not possible," he said to himself. "It's just not possible." But then, he thought ruefully, at Creepe Hall anything was possible. Without the photographs, though, no one would believe what he said about his "new" relations. They would think he was telling stories, like Darren and Damien. So he decided there and then that he wouldn't say anything. It would be his secret.

He gazed again at the beautiful moon lamp and pictured how it would look on his bedside cabinet at home. He'd put it where his TV was now, where he could see it clearly every night, when he was lying in bed. He'd been given another gift too, he remembered – from Uncle Vladimir – and he took it out now from his jacket pocket. It was a small and rather dusty book called *The Layman's Guide to Chiroptera*. Reading the title, Oliver smiled and shook his head. "Bats," he murmured – and that seemed to sum up Creepe Hall and its inhabitants perfectly.

RETURN TO CREEPE HALL

Alan Durant

Returning to Creepe Hall for the holidays, Oliver is delighted to find the Creepe family as weird and wonderful as ever. Uncle Vladimir, the fiery vampire, batty boffin Uncle Franklin, Werebadger, Mummy and the twins Con and Can all play their parts in a fantastic new adventure for Oliver, involving body-snatchers, rotten fangs, a snow machine and the extraordinary Creepe-creation, Cleopatra!

"A rollicking read to sink your fangs into."
Young Telegraph

JAKE'S MAGIC

Alan Durant

All Jake wants is a pet, but it seems as though his wish will never come true. Then one day a small, stray tabby appears and the magic begins!

"Delightful... The characterisation is excellent and the line drawings match the text perfectly. This should find a welcome place in a class library as well as on the home bookshelf."
The School Librarian

"Alan Durant's pleasantly low key style makes this story particularly effective."
Children's Books of the Year

SMART GIRLS

Robert Leeson

They're witty, they're wise – you can't pull the wool over these girls' eyes!

"Five folk tales from across the world simply and skilfully retold... The stories are lively and funny." *Gillian Cross, The Daily Telegraph*

"Entertaining, thought provoking and a source of invaluable learning." *Books for Keeps*

Shortlisted for the Guardian Children's Fiction Award

THE TIME SAILORS
Ian Whybrow

Edward loves the old brown photo of Grandad Wilson and his friend Futter when they were boys. They are pictured standing by a river with an oar and an old-fashioned pram, and between them, as if just floating in the air, is a cloth cap. What's it doing there? Who does it belong to? Well, now the mystery is about to be solved at last, as Grandad Wilson takes Edward on a magical trip back to the day in 1919 when the picture was taken!

MORE WALKER PAPERBACKS
For You to Enjoy